This Walker book
belongs to:

_____

_____

For Abel
May you see well
and hear happily!

First published 2011 as *Ancient Egypt: Tales of Gods and Pharaohs*
by Walker Books Ltd, 87 Vauxhall Walk, London SE11 5HJ

This edition published 2020

2 4 6 8 10 9 7 5 3 1

© 2011, 2020 Marcia Williams

The right of Marcia Williams to be identified as author/illustrator of this work
has been asserted by her in accordance with the Copyright, Designs and Patents Act 1988

This book has been typeset in Berylium and Marcia

Printed and bound in Great Britain by CPI Group (UK) Ltd, Croydon CRO 4YY

British Library Cataloguing in Publication Data:
a catalogue record for this book is available from the British Library

ISBN 978-1-4063-8403-1

www.walker.co.uk

ANCIENT EGYPT
GODS, PHARAOHS

and Cats!

Marcia Williams

WALKER BOOKS
AND SUBSIDIARIES
LONDON · BOSTON · SYDNEY · AUCKLAND

CONTENTS

DEAR READER

Allow me to introduce myself: I am Rami, the cat. Many moons ago, I was the pet of the great Egyptian god Ra, the Shining One. Now, thanks to the power given to me by Ra, I am a teller of tales. I am about to share with you my favourite stories of gods and pharaohs – the stories of Ancient Egypt.

They come from a time and place so rich in mystery and imagination that you are likely to be blown away!

Everyone knows that cats have nine lives and I am on my ninth life now, so these are the final tales I will tell before I rejoin the great god Ra.

These are the stories closest to my little, feline heart. They have been told and retold throughout the ages, changing with each retelling, but they are no less wondrous for that.

So, come with me. Let me transport you back to a time when gods walked upon this earth!

And as we used to say in Ancient Egypt, "May you see well and hear happily!"

Rami

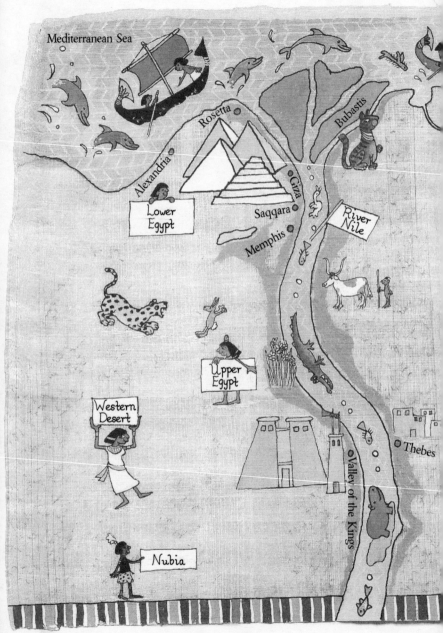

Mediterranean Sea

Rosetta

Bubastis

Alexandria

Giza

Saqqara

Lower Egypt

River Nile

Memphis

Upper Egypt

Western Desert

Thebes

Valley of the Kings

Nubia

10

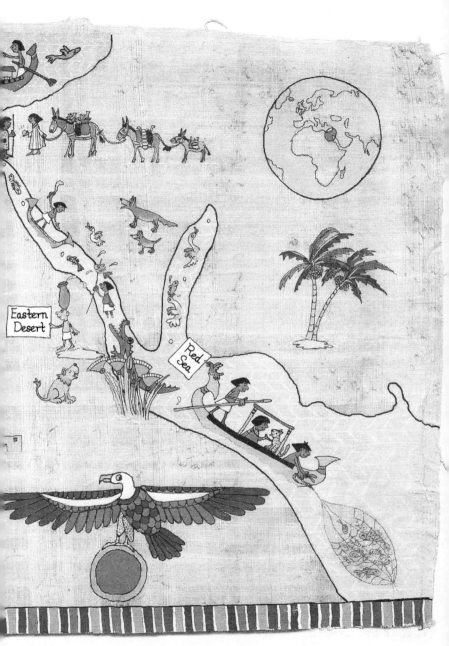

Eastern
Desert

Red
Sea

Chapter One
IN THE BEGINNING

So my little ticklers, if you are curled up comfortably we will begin...

In Ancient Egypt many different tales were told about how the world was created, but one thing everyone agreed on was that in the beginning there was only chaos and the deep, dark water of Nun. Out of the chaos something came into being and this thing was called Zep Tepi, which meant "the first time". In some tales the being was Ra, the Shining One, my master.

Ra was wonderfully powerful. He had a

Secret Name, which gave him the ability to bring

anything into being with just a word or a glance!

The first thing that Ra brought forth was an island that rose out of the deep, dark water. Now Ra, the Shining One, had somewhere to place his feet and so he became the first god to stand on the land of Egypt.

Ra looked about him and saw that he was alone, and that the land he stood on was barren. He felt lonely and sad. Using his Secret Name, Ra brought forth Shu, the god of air, and Tefnut, the goddess of rain. Then came Geb, the god of the

earth, and Nut, the goddess of the sky. Now the land and sky were divided, as were the day and night, and rain fell upon the land to make it fertile. Ra looked at his creation and smiled to himself.

"I am indeed Ra, the very powerful and Shining One. A creator without compare!" he said with pride.

Ra thought some more about the land he had created and he saw that there were many gods, but that the land he stood on was still empty. He whispered his Secret Name once more and Hapi, the great River Nile that flows through Egypt, was born. A fine river that ran clear and strong, but whose waters were empty – until Ra whispered his Secret Name again. Fish swam in the deep and shallow waters, crocodiles glided among tall reeds and waterfowl swam on the surface. The waters of Hapi flowed contentedly and Ra clapped his hands in delight.

"This is good," he thought. "But the land still looks very empty and I am lonely."

This time Ra opened his arms very wide and closed his eyes. He whispered his Secret Name with a force so great that it gave life to men, women and all the things on the land of Egypt, both great and small. When Ra opened his eyes and looked about him even he – the great god

Ra – was astonished by all that he had created.

The land was clothed in lush vegetation,

and around and above and beneath this canopy

were creatures of every colour and description,

including mankind – the most wondrous creature of all!

"Wow!" cried Ra, the Shining One, in a voice that echoed around the whole land. "You are so very welcome."

All were awed by this mighty god who had given them life and all – both great and small – bowed down before him. Only one, I the cat named Rami, dared to come forward and jump on the great god's knee!

"Shall I be your special favourite?" I purred.

"We'll see," replied Ra, stroking my soft fur.

"Maybe," said Ra, as my tail tickled his nose.

"Definitely!" he sneezed, as I curled into a warm ball on his lap. "The cat named Rami is Ra's favourite, and to him and to all his kin, I give nine lives!"

"This is as it should be," I purred, a very satisfied cat. "For I am, and always shall be, irresistible!"

Then, as Ra loved the land he had created so much that he didn't want to return to the sky, he whispered his Secret Name one last time and took on the shape of a man. He had decided to become the first pharaoh of Egypt, so that he could care for his creation.

For many years, Ra ruled the land wisely and man and beast learned to live in harmony with each other. Every year the River Nile rose up and flooded the fields, leaving behind a rich silt that helped the crops to grow. There was peace and plenty for all during the long reign of Ra.

And I, Rami the cat, lived a pampered life!

Chapter Two
ISIS AND THE COBRA

My next tale may seem sad but be of good cheer for gods, like cats, never really die – well, not for ages and ages!

So chin on paws and hear most attentively!

In the reign of Ra, Nut, the goddess of the sky, and Geb, the god of the earth had a daughter – the goddess, Isis. Isis grew into a beautiful, clever and wise young woman. She had two younger brothers, Osiris and Seth, but Osiris was Ra's favourite and the heir to his crown. This pleased Isis greatly, for as well as being clever, she was also ambitious.

"If we marry, I'll be your queen!" She smiled, blowing Osiris a kiss.

"Good plan," he replied as he caught the kiss. "Let's keep the power of Egypt in the family."

So she married Osiris, her brother (which was quite usual in Ancient Egypt), and he was her one true love. As time passed, Ra's human form grew old and frail and the land of Egypt, which had once prospered under his rule, became scorched and barren. The river no longer flooded and made the fields fertile, the crops no longer stood proud

in the fields. Children went hungry and parents grew discontented and quarrelsome. Ra, who had once been honoured by all, became nothing but a weak old man in the eyes of his people. Instead of being cheered as he passed through the land, Ra was now mocked.

"Where's your great power gone now, Pharaoh?" they'd cry. "The grain is withering in the fields and your people are starving."

Like many elderly people, Ra lived in the memories of his past glory and was deaf to their cries. He would wave a kingly wave and hobble on his way.

"Yuck! He's dribbling!" cried the children.

"He's as useless as a baby!" jeered the women.

"Time you went back to the skies old man, and take that mangy cat with you," cried a man so short-sighted that he was unable to see that I, Rami, was very much in my prime!

Ra did not want to give Osiris his crown, for in his rheumy old eyes he was still the all-powerful god Ra, the Shining One. He had given birth to Egypt and without him the world would have remained in darkness and chaos for ever. Even the honeyed words of Isis would not persuade him to let go of his power.

"You are the greatest, dearest Ra," she soothed. "There will never be a pharaoh to match you but your people want you to rest now and take your place in the heavens."

"I like being pharaoh," he replied tetchily. "It's my right."

Isis looked across the land of Egypt and knew that something must be done before it became desert and every child starved.

"I'll find out his Secret Name," she whispered to Osiris. "Then I'll have power over him."

"Never! Even now he is too canny to let you know that," replied her husband.

"Just you watch me, my little love." Isis smiled, planting a kiss on her true love's nose.

Isis knew that Osiris was right. She would never persuade Ra to give up his Secret Name or

the crown, so she decided to use her magic powers against him. She spent many days forming her
plan until she was finally ready to put it into action.
When Ra next went on one of his walks across the
land, Isis followed close behind. When Ra dribbled
on the ground (as he always did) Isis waited until
he'd passed out of sight, then she secretly formed
the damp sand into the shape of a cobra.

"You will carry the venom of darkness," she

whispered in its sandy ear.

The next day, Ra again took a turn around his land, passing the same spot as the day before. When he passed the sand-shaped cobra, the shining light of his eye fell on it and brought the serpent to life.

"I don't remember creating you," exclaimed Ra, as the huge cobra reared up in front of him.

"Well, you'll remember my bite!" it hissed –

and sank its fangs into Ra's arm, releasing its venom into the old man's veins.

Ra cried out in agony as the venom spread and the pain grew like fire in his limbs. His legs buckled beneath him and his eyes gradually dimmed.

"Is there not one god who will help me?" he pleaded as he was carried to his bed. "Where's Osiris, surely he will save me?"

"Sorry, only Isis can help you," Osiris told the old man. "I will fetch her for you."

Isis came to Ra's bedside and held the dying pharaoh's hand. She offered to heal him if he told her his Secret Name. Ra was delirious with pain and spoke many names, but none of them was his Secret Name of power.

"If I mix your Secret Name with my magic, I can cure you," promised Isis.

"I am Khepera at dawn, Ra at noon and Tum in the evening," said Ra.

But Isis knew that none of
these was the name that
gave Ra his great power
and she used her magic instead
to increase the pain of the
venom that coursed through
his body. The agony became unbearable and Ra
called Isis to come close to him. The Secret Name
passed from his heart to hers and Isis felt the
power of Ra enter her. Only then did she bid the
serpent's venom leave Ra's body and at last the
great god was at peace.

Ra begged Isis to return his Secret Name, but she refused and so became the most powerful goddess in Egypt. Without his Secret Name, Ra could no longer reign on Earth so he took his place in the heavens

and travelled across the sky in the likeness of the sun. He became known as Amen Ra and I, his beautiful cat Rami, travelled with him.

At night Ra passed through the underworld, called the Duat. As dawn rose he returned to the heavens, taking with him the spirits of the dead who had won a place in his heavenly kingdom. I did love Ra, but I found the endless journeying irksome.

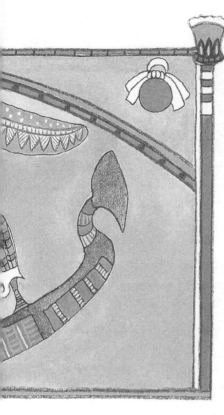

"Where are the fish?" I howled. "How can I sit on your knee when you're always journeying?"

"Stop complaining or it's back to the Duat for you," replied Ra, who wished to keep me beside him until the end of time.

"Sorry, Ra, but I'm off to live my nine lives on Earth," I purred, giving him one last rub of the legs, before leaping from his heavenly ship and diving back down towards the earth.

"You'll come scurrying back when you run out of lives!" Ra shouted after me.

Meanwhile, in the land of Egypt, Osiris became the new pharaoh and Isis his queen. They cared well for their people, teaching them many things – including not to eat each other, which the great hunger caused by Ra had tempted them to do.

Osiris and Isis built a magnificent temple for Amen Ra in their new city of Thebes and it was never forgotten that he was Ra, the Shining One, creator of all Egypt. Isis turned out to be a great queen and used the power of Ra wisely. She was a wonderful role model for the women of Egypt

and showed them how to weave, bake and brew beer. Osiris and Isis lived happily in Thebes for many years and their happiness was completed by the birth of a son, Horus.

As for me, when I jumped from Ra's boat I

fell through the heavens until I eventually landed

with a splash in the River Nile! I tussled with a

crocodile and sadly lost the first of my lives. I

knew I had eight more lives to live so I decided to

live them in great comfort in the palace of Pharaoh

Osiris and Queen Isis!

So you see, my ticklers, it wasn't too sad...

And I would definitely have saved Ra from the cobra. If only I hadn't been asleep in the shade of a pomegranate tree!

Chapter Three
SETH THE EVIL ONE

I would not honour evil Seth with a tale – but unfortunately, my last story leads to this next one!

So, chin on paws and off we go.

The reign of Pharaoh Osiris and Queen Isis was popular across the whole land of Egypt, except with Seth, Osiris's jealous younger brother. In Seth's mind Osiris was not the rightful pharaoh – he thought that the honour should have fallen to him.

"After all," he said to his band of unsavoury friends, "I am both the best-looking and most in need of Egypt's riches."

"Well, it would certainly go well with us if you had some riches." The evil ones grinned.

Most of Seth's waking hours were spent planning how he might steal his brother's crown. Isis suspected Seth of a plot and warned Osiris to be careful, making sure that her husband was always guarded well.

Osiris found it hard to believe his younger brother would ever harm him. He seemed oblivious of the danger and unaware of Seth's

spies, who lurked in every shadow of the pharaoh's palace.

At night, Seth lay in bed muttering curses into the darkness. "Death, sickness and weakness to you," he'd whisper. "O my most un-beloved pharaoh. May the milk curdle inside my nephew Horus and may his limbs shrivel and drop off."

In the presence of Osiris however, Seth was all charm and good wishes.

"O, most beloved brother," he would say. "May the light of Ra shine on you, your honoured queen and your most precious baby, Horus. May you live for endless years and may your crown always stay fixed to your fine head

– until, of course, it passes to your son, Horus."

"You're too kind," replied Osiris.

"You're too slippery, brother Seth," whispered Isis. And my hackles as I sat on her knee were seen to rise!

Finally, after months of plotting, Seth invited Osiris to a banquet with some of his wickedest friends.

"A boys' night in," he said to Osiris. "A bit of music, some dancing, food and wine. Come, brother! It'll be fun!"

Suspecting a plot, Isis begged Osiris not to go but he ignored her.

"He's my brother. All will be well," he reassured her.

The party was everything Seth had promised. There was music, delicious food, wonderful wine

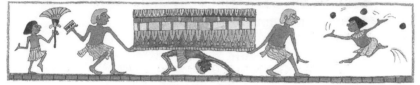

and good – if somewhat bawdy – company. After the feasting, Seth announced a competition. A beautiful casket inlaid with many precious stones was carried in – a gift from Seth to anyone who could fit themselves inside.

"A mere trifle for any man nimble enough to snuggle themselves in," announced Seth, to a fanfare of trumpets.

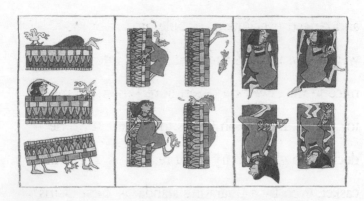

"Fantastic, what a brilliant idea," laughed his guests ... including Osiris.

Every one of Seth's friends tried to wriggle, squish or squeeze themselves into the beautiful trunk but to no avail. They were either too big

and bulged over like great Nile hippos or they were too small and vanished into its interior like mice in the jaws of a desert lion! When it came for the great Pharaoh Osiris to take his turn, he decided to give it a try for it really was a very fine casket, even by a pharaoh's standards. First Osiris slid one foot in and then the other, then he held onto the sides and lowered himself down.

"By all the gods of Egypt!" he exclaimed. "This casket is a perfect fit!"

"What a surprise," cried Seth, not at all surprised. "You must keep it, dear brother!" And he slammed the lid down. "Consider it a little gift from me, in return for the crown of Egypt –

which is now *mine!*" he declared in triumph.

Seth's wicked friends threw the casket into the Nile. It had become nothing more than Osiris's coffin and it floated off towards the sea, bobbing up and down, disturbing only the odd crocodile or hippopotamus.

Queen Isis was heartbroken at the loss of her

husband, her one true love, and she shed endless tears of pain and sorrow. She was desperate to find his body as she believed that without it, he would never be able to pass safely into the next world.

"What can we do?" she wept to little Horus. "We must find his body or he will never take his place as King of the Underworld."

"Waaah!" cried baby Horus, which was as
much as any baby can say.

Isis knew that Seth would come for Horus
next and was nervous of leaving him but she
had to find Osiris's body.

"Keep him hidden from his Uncle Seth!"
she pleaded to his nursemaids and guards
before she left.

After many weeks of fruitless searching, Isis
reached the city of Byblos where, with the help of
her magic, she discovered Osiris's coffin. It had
been washed ashore and lay on the banks of the
Nile under a tamarisk bush.

"No wonder this tamarisk smells so sweet,"
sighed Isis, her arms clutching the coffin.

"Come," she said to her servants. "We must

hurry back to Thebes before Seth gets wind of our discovery."

Osiris's body was carried aboard Isis's ship and she set sail for Thebes with all the speed her oarsmen could muster. Alas, rumours of her return reached Thebes ahead of her and when she landed Seth's spies were waiting. Silent steps followed her to where she hid the coffin.

"First I must prepare your tomb, my love, so

just stay hidden here a while," Isis whispered. "You will be safe."

But there were no guards strong enough to

hold back a raging Seth. While Isis prepared the tomb, Seth's spies led him to the coffin.

"Have you come back to haunt me, brother?" he cried, kicking the coffin so hard that it split in two.

Then and there, he took up his sword and chopped his brother's body into fourteen pieces. Gathering them up, he mounted his horse and galloped away, scattering the pieces all across the land of Egypt.

"Now try haunting me!" he snarled. "Not even

your beloved Isis will be able to stick you back together."

Hearing what had befallen her husband's remains, poor Isis set out once more to look for his body parts. After weeks of searching she

managed to find all but one piece.

"I had a special fondness for that bit," she wept. "But I must bury you without it, in case Seth finds you again."

"Burp!" went a very full fish, as it sank deep into the waters of the Nile.

To protect Osiris from Seth, Isis buried him in thirteen different places. And in each place Isis used the power of Ra to conjure a whole body. So finally, the spirit of Osiris passed into the Duat,

where he became King of the Dead and his wicked brother, Seth, became pharaoh of Egypt, which was far more than he deserved!

"I will have my revenge," a voice roared from the underworld.

"No chance," laughed Seth, jumping up and

down with delight. "Now I'm pharaoh, as well as a god, I will be twice as evil so you don't stand a chance, brother!"

What did I tell you, my ticklers? Purrfectly frightful! And he does not improve.

So, join me ... if you dare!

Chapter Four
HORUS THE AVENGER

Yes, it's the cat's own truth, Seth gets worse, much worse!

So gather your courage, curl up tight and read on.

Although Seth had crowned himself pharaoh of Egypt, he knew that the crown really belonged to his young nephew, Horus. And while Horus lived, the crown did not feel secure on Seth's head. As the days passed, he imagined Horus growing older and stronger. He became convinced that one day, Horus would arrive at the palace to avenge his father's death and take back the crown of Egypt.

"We don't want that nasty Horus stealing you, do we?" he said, addressing his crown. "We'll just

have to kill him, won't we my precious?" He
smiled. "While he's still a little blob of a thing and
easy to dispatch!"

Isis knew that Seth would not rest until he
had killed Horus, so she kept him well-guarded
on a floating island in the River Nile.

"You are safe from your nasty Uncle Seth here,"
she would say. "But never venture off the island
without me."

"No, Mama," he always replied. "I wouldn't

dream of it, but one day, when I am big and strong, I will avenge my father's death."

At the thought of her husband, Isis would weep, for not an hour passed by without her feeling the pain of his loss. And always I, the cat Rami, stayed close and comforted her.

"I know, my son," she replied. "But the time has not yet come."

One night, there was a great wind that blew the floating island against the banks of the Nile.

As the island bumped against the land, wicked
Seth was waiting and crossed quietly onto it. He
took the shape of a great, black scorpion and
crawled into Horus's bedroom. Scuttling across to
the young boy's bed, he stung him with the most
vicious venom before retreating into the darkness.

All night long Horus screamed in agony, for the pain of the scorpion bite was a terrible thing. Isis used all her power and magic to try to heal him but by morning Horus was on the brink of death.

"My magic has no power against such evil," wept Isis. "Wise god Thoth, please come and heal my son. Isn't it enough that I have already lost his father?"

Thoth, the god of wisdom, came to Isis and comforted her as best he could. As the life finally

seeped from Horus, Thoth reassured her that,
although he could not cure her son, she would
see him again.

"He is the rightful pharaoh – he will live again,"

promised Thoth.

Meanwhile, the spirit of Horus had passed into the Duat. He had been called there by Osiris, his father, King of the Dead. Osiris wished to prepare his son to fight Seth and get vengeance for both their deaths.

"You will avenge us and I will prepare you for the task," said Osiris, as he welcomed his son.

"Do not doubt it, Dad." Horus smiled, delighted to be out of pain.

From that day on, Osiris coached his son in

the skills of battle – not an hour passed without another lesson. Horus grew in skill and strength until eventually, he was ready to fight Seth.

"I think I'm well prepared, Dad," he said, flexing his muscles.

"Never underestimate your uncle's power," warned his father.

"I am up for anything he can throw at me!" Horus laughed with the confidence of a trained fighter.

Amen Ra carried Horus to the land of the living in his heavenly ship. He too warned Horus of Seth's strength and evil.

"You may need more than weapons to fight

Seth," he said.

"Don't worry about me, I do have the odd magic power," replied Horus, who had forgotten the pain of Seth's evil venom.

Unfortunately for Horus, Seth's spies had not been idle all this time and when Horus disembarked from Amen Ra's boat, Seth was ready and waiting. Seth was disguised as a wild boar and as Horus's feet touched the land of Egypt, Seth charged at him and aimed a

bolt of fire straight into Horus's eyes.

"It's Seth!" cried out Horus, but it was too late
– he was blinded. He was unable to fight back. He
roared with pain and anger.

"I can't see. All my training was in vain," wailed
Horus.

"No, Horus, you will
get your revenge," said
Amen Ra. "I'll heal you

and you will fight again," he continued, scooping
up the injured youth and carrying him to the
heavens. "You must rest in the dark and I will
apply many herbs and much magic."

Horus tried not sink into despair while his eyes

healed. But even with the great god Amen Ra as his healer, it was weeks before the bandages were removed from his eyes and Horus could finally see again.

When at last Horus left the safety of Amen Ra's care and returned to Earth, he was much more careful, for he now knew that Seth could come at

him from anywhere and in any guise.

For weeks Horus stalked his enemy, but every time he thought he had Seth cornered, his wily uncle had escaped. Horus grew angry and frustrated, but he would not give up.

"What I need is an army," he decided. "I'll talk to Mum, she'll help me gather one together."

So with the help of Isis, Horus gathered a great army and chased Seth up the River Nile.

"Come on, guys, he's out there somewhere," cried Horus.

Horus looked into the eye of every crocodile and wild beast that skulked on the banks of the Nile, but he did not spy Seth. Maybe he wasn't out there after all; maybe he had returned to Thebes.

"We'll just sail upriver for one more day," Horus decided. "If we find nothing, we'll return home and flush him out of his palace."

Then, as they reached the island of Elephantine, Seth appeared in the shape of a vast red hippo-potamus. It was fearful indeed to behold!

"Let there come a raging tempest and a mighty flood against my enemies!" cried Seth, the hippopotamus.

As he spoke, the wind began to rage, the waves
rose and a great blackness fell over Egypt. Only
the boat of Horus gleamed in the dark as the
gigantic hippopotamus opened its jaws to crush
him. Horus felt its saliva flowing towards him
and he could smell the great beast's fetid breath.
Quickly, he took on the likeness of a young giant.
Horus drew back his arm and, with every bit of
strength he could muster, he cast a long harpoon.
He threw it with such force that it travelled

through the roof of Seth's mouth and into his

brain. The red hippopotamus sank dead into the

Nile and the darkness vanished.

As Horus sailed back to Thebes the banks
were crowded with cheering Egyptians, for both
the gods and the people rejoiced at the victory of

Horus the Avenger. Horus took his rightful place on the throne of Egypt and peace returned to the country. Isis still wept for Osiris, for he was her one true love, but she was content that his death had been avenged and that her son, the rightful heir, now sat on the throne of Egypt.

And the cat, Rami, my ticklers, continued to sit on the knee of Isis and feed off the finest fish from the Nile.

Chapter Five
PHARAOH ZOSER AND THE GREAT FAMINE

You may want to pause now but my time is running out so I must continue.

When you're ready, join me. Chin on paws and off we go!

After the reign of Horus, the great gods decided to leave the day-to-day ruling of Egypt to mortals.

"After all," said Ra, the Shining One, "we

have been ruling Egypt since the beginning of
time. It's time we stayed in the heavens and
behaved like the great gods we are."

"O Ra, what a splendid idea!" cried the gods in
unison. "We were beginning to think you'd never
let us take a break!"

So Horus was the last of the ancient gods to
rule Egypt and a man was made a mortal pharaoh.

Zoser, like other mortal pharaohs, was

worshipped by the people of Egypt as if he were a god, but everyone knew that the ancient gods still came first. Beautiful temples were built to honour them, sacrifices were made to please them and they were always consulted in times of hardship. Of course, there was a danger that a mortal pharaoh might suffer from pride and put himself above the ancient gods – but most pharaohs were far too wise ... until the

time of Zoser!

"Am I the greatest?" Pharaoh Zoser would ask his courtiers.

"You are great," they would reply. "In fact, you are pretty, jolly great. Indeed, we would say you are jolly, pretty, jolly great. But you are not actually quite as great as Ra, the Shining One and the other ancient gods."

"No, no. You are absolutely right," Zoser replied for the first few years of his reign. But as time went on, power went to Zoser's head and he began to believe that he really was an ancient god with all the attendant powers.

"You know what, Vizier Imhotep?" Zoser announced one day. "I have come to realize that I am pretty godlike and I think I should have a very big tomb built for myself. I want everyone to

remember me when I'm gone. So see to it, Vizier
Imhotep, will you?"

I, the cat, Rami, who by now had lived in the
palace for many years, raised my hackles and hissed
in disapproval.

"Treason," shouted Pharaoh Zoser. "Strangle
that cat!"

And so I lost another life – in an instant!

"Actually," Zoser continued, hardly blinking an
eye at the death of the palace cat, "I want you to

build me a tomb that rises higher than any temple to the ancient gods of Egypt, so that my people remember where their loyalty lies."

"O, Pharaoh, I love a challenge!" declared Imhotep. "But maybe just a few metres lower than the highest temple? It would be more stylish and less likely to anger the gods."

"Absolutely not!" snarled Zoser. "And if you want that ugly head of yours to stay attached to your body, I suggest you get on with my very large tomb!"

Imhotep could not disobey his pharaoh and so he started work on the most extravagant build Egypt had ever seen. Zoser was an impatient man and every day he would ask, "Is my tomb ready yet?"

"It is progressing, great Pharaoh Zoser,"

Imhotep would reply, until eventually he was able to declare that Zoser's burial place was ready for inspection.

"O Pharaoh come, it awaits you." He smiled. "I think it will please you, great and mighty Zoser."

Well, it did indeed please Pharaoh Zoser, for his tomb was so outstandingly beautiful it took his and every other Egyptian's breath away! It was a step pyramid built at Saqqara, on the edge of the desert – the very first pyramid ever to be built. The outside was covered in white limestone and during

the day it glinted in the sunlight. At night it looked
like a stairway to the heavens.

"Will it last?" asked Zoser.

"Until the end of time," promised Imhotep,
stroking the kitten Rami that lay hidden in his robe.
(I was starting my third life already.)

Inside, wonderful etchings and carvings decorated the walls leading to Zoser's burial chamber. There were many false burial chambers to confuse any tomb robbers, but inside the actual burial chamber hieroglyphs praised the might of Zoser across the ceiling and on every wall. Never before had such a large stone monument been built, not even for the great god Ra, creator of all Egypt. There was no doubt that for as long as it stood,

Pharaoh Zoser would be remembered, which made him very, very happy.

"Not bad, Imhotep," Zoser said grudgingly. "You may keep your head."

The people of Egypt came to admire Zoser's magnificent pyramid and to praise the pharaoh who had ordered it to be built.

"Wow! Pharaoh Zoser is the best," they cried. "Let us worship him, for his tomb is mightier

than any temple!"

As time passed, the people of Egypt began to neglect the ancient gods and worshipped Pharaoh Zoser instead. Zoser, of course, was delighted and had quite forgotten that he was a mere mortal. The temples built in honour of the ancient gods were crumbling and only a few remaining priests were left to remind the people of Egypt where their true duty lay.

"Come – help me repair the mighty temple of Thoth," cried one. "His festival is due."

"Sorry, we're off to worship at Zoser's tomb," came the reply.

Zoser ordered Imhotep to add a touch more gold and a few more precious jewels to the carvings inside the tomb.

"After all, it should be fit for a god." He smiled.

In the heavens the anger of the gods rumbled.

Something must be done to punish this pharaoh who had put himself above them! The next year the Nile did not rise and flood the fields, leaving its rich deposits and making the land fertile. Farmers tried to plant their seeds in the dry desert, but the crops failed and the people of Egypt had to live on the grain that had been stored from other years.

"Just one bag of grain each," they were warned, for nobody knew how long the famine would last.

"Next year the Nile is bound to rise!" said
Pharaoh Zoser, who had a rich store of food and
was not overly concerned by the plight of his people.
The following year, the Nile failed to rise again

and the stores of grain were empty. Zoser's people turned to him for help, but he was only a man and did not have the power to raise the waters of the Nile – however much they begged.

"Health to you, O Pharaoh. Your people need food," they pleaded. "Actually, your people need food really, really urgently!"

"For some reason the Nile will not obey my divine powers today," said Zoser. "I'll try again tomorrow."

Day after day, the waters of the Nile receded

until at last, Zoser appealed to the gods. "Dear gods, please help us. Please!" he begged.

But the gods heard no apology from Zoser and knew that he was not truly repentant.

"Did we hear a prayer or even an apology? No, we think not," they said, turning their backs on Egypt.

For seven years the Nile failed to flood. Farmland turned to desert and the Egyptians

starved. Neighbour robbed neighbour, children were left to die and fists were raised at Zoser.

"You're our pharaoh. Do something!" they cried.

Zoser was finally beginning to realize that he did not have the power of the gods, even if he

did think of himself as most godly! He was pow-
erless to help his angry people and even his own
food stores were now depleted. Finally, he ordered
Imhotep to go and consult with Thoth, the god
of wisdom.

"Find out which god directs the flood … and
hurry!" he ordered.

"I'll try, but I'm weak with hunger and hardly
able to walk," replied Imhotep.

Thoth told Imhotep that Zoser must travel to
Elephantine and pray to the god Khnemu.

"Only Khnemu has power over the Nile," said Thoth. "And there are no guarantees. He's angry – we are all angry!"

Zoser made haste and with a small retinue and a few gifts, he took the royal barge to the island of Elephantine. There was so little water left in the Nile that the barge scraped along the bottom. At times Zoser's slaves had to get out and drag the boat across its muddy bed, but finally they made it to the island.

Zoser called forth Khnemu and prayed to be forgiven for neglecting the gods.

"I bring you gifts and apologies," he said.

"I can see the gifts, but I can't hear the apology," said Khnemu.

"I am but a grain of sand compared to the great god Khnemu," implored Zoser.

"Better … but still not good enough," said Khnemu, turning his back on Pharaoh Zoser.

"You are right, Khnemu. I am not worthy of

your forgiveness. I have been a complete and utter idiot. I have not behaved as a pharaoh should and I am certainly not in the least godlike. Please – let me build a temple for the great god Khnemu, grander even than my own tomb!"

"You're almost there. Try once more and I might forgive you," said Khnemu.

Zoser bent his old and creaking knees before Khnemu. "Put it this way Khnemu, you are a mighty god and I am an insignificant little pharaoh who is rather hungry. My people are suffering because of my outrageous pride. I am truly sorry and in dire need of your divine intervention!"

"Hmmm. I do believe you have seen the error of your ways," said Khnemu, satisfied at last. "Let the Nile rise up and the people of Egypt be fed!"

Gradually, Egypt returned to being a land of

plenty, but neither Pharaoh Zoser, nor his people, ever again risked neglecting the ancient gods.

As for me, Rami, after the death of Imhotep, I migrated to Nubia where there was a plague of rats. My fur remained sleek, my belly full and my seven remaining lives intact! Until there was a nasty incident with a lion, which reduced my lives to six. I have long held the belief that lions, being overgrown cats, should not eat their own kind. I shall take it up with Ra when I finally return to the heavens.

Chapter Six

HATSHEPSUT, A GREAT QUEEN FOR EGYPT

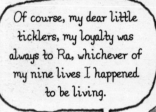

Of course, my dear little ticklers, my loyalty was always to Ra, whichever of my nine lives I happened to be living.

However, he did have one rival, Pharaoh Hatshepsut – I stayed with her for three whole lives!

Although Amen Ra had decided to hand over the daily running of Egypt to a mortal pharaoh, he still liked to keep a close eye on his creation. One day, he looked down on the people of Egypt and it came into his head that they should be ruled by a queen.

"Yes, my Egypt, it's time for a feminine touch," he announced to no one in particular. "A woman

will bring new wisdoms. But who is worthy to be
the first ruling queen of Egypt?"

Ra pondered on the matter for some time and
finally chose Ahmes, wife of Pharaoh Thutmose, to

be the mother of the first queen of Egypt.

"There is no woman alive who is quite special enough," he smiled to himself, "but with a little bit of godly help we will have a fine queen! Old Thoth will help me, he loves a bit of midnight magic."

The following night, Amen Ra and Thoth went to the palace of Thutmose and cast a spell upon the household so that every living thing slept. Then Ra entered the chamber of Ahmes, bathing the room in light. As he placed himself beside her

the couch rose up, so that it was neither on the earth nor in the heavens. Ra held a sweet perfume to Ahmes's nostrils and the breath of a new life passed into her.

After nine months, Ahmes gave birth to a baby
girl named Hatshepsut. All Egypt rejoiced, for
Ra put it into the minds of the people that even
though this was a girl baby, she was special and
would do great things for Egypt. Then, once again,
a great sleep fell upon the palace while Ra visited
the child. This time he took with him Hathor,
the goddess of love, and her seven daughters
who weave the web of life for all newborns. Ra
gave Hatshepsut the kiss of power and the Hathors

wove the golden web of her life so that she would be a great queen. All the while, the palace slept unaware of the magical things happening all around them.

As Hatshepsut grew, she became everything Ra had hoped for. She was wise, clever, funny and very fond of cats – especially her own cat, Rami! As soon as she was able, Hatshepsut took her place beside her earthly father, Pharaoh Thutmose, and learned how to care for Egypt and its people. Pharaoh Thutmose knew in his heart that Hatshepsut would inherit his crown.

"You're a girl and the people may not like it, so you'll just have to be patient," he advised.

"Yes, Father. Of course I will." Hatshepsut smiled.

"Be kind to your people. Be fair to your people. Be generous to your people," Pharaoh Thutmose advised.

"Yes, Father. Of course I will." Hatshepsut smiled.

"Be as kind to your people as you are to that cat of yours and then you won't go far wrong."

"Enough, Father! Of course I will. You know I will. I will, I will, I will!" she laughed.

"Unless of course, you behave like Pharaoh Zoser

and place yourself above the ancient gods – but you are too wise to behave like that," her father continued.

"Oh Father, go to bed and rest your poor head!" she cried.

Hatshepsut was only twelve years old when her father died. She was very sad, for he had been a wonderful father and a wise teacher.

As was the tradition in Egypt, Hatshepsut married her half-brother Thutmose II and became his queen. She knew far more than her husband about ruling Egypt and made most of the decisions of state while Thutmose spent most of his time hunting.

After fifteen years, Thutmose died and instead of allowing the throne to go to the next male heir – as was the law of Egypt – Hatshepsut

made herself pharaoh.

"Don't argue with me," she advised her ministers. "You know perfectly well I have been the power behind the throne for the past fifteen years. The only difference now is that it's official, so pass the beard of office to me!"

I sat on her knee and purred with pride.

To show her people that she was indeed their leader, Hatshepsut had herself depicted on the palace walls in the traditional king's kilt and crown, complete with fake beard! This was not to trick the people into thinking she was a man, but to show her importance as the first female pharaoh of Egypt.

"Actually, I think the beard rather suits me – I might wear it every day," Pharaoh Hatshepsut teased.

"O mighty Pharaoh," her ministers cried. "Is that wise? Not even Ra, the Shining One, wore the beard of office every day."

"Ah, but I'm not a god. I'm a woman and the first one to be pharaoh of Egypt, so I think I'd like to look the part!" She winked.

Hatshepsut and Amen Ra were both very happy for they had always known that this was Hatshepsut's destiny. She ruled for twenty years and, unlike many previous pharaohs, she brought

peace to the land of Egypt. She chose her ministers wisely and together they encouraged the restoration and building of many fine monuments, developed trade and carefully managed Egypt's farming and resources. Egypt flourished under the rule of its first female pharaoh and everyone mourned her passing.

"I knew a female pharaoh was a good idea," said Ra, to no one in particular. "Shame she had to die. Still, I think my Pharaoh Hatshepsut will

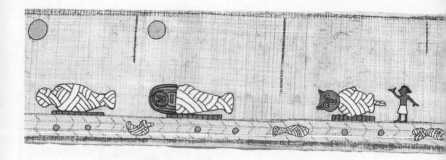

be remembered as one of the first great women

in history."

And indeed she is!

With Hatshepsut's passing I lost another life, for as was traditional in ancient Egypt, I was most cruelly murdered and then embalmed alongside my mistress. I would have travelled with her to the next world as intended, but I still had three lives to live and I am not one to tolerate waste!

Chapter Seven
PRINCE THUTMOSE AND THE SPHINX

Well, my ticklers, chin on paws – it's time for another tale.

A friend of mine told me this one, for I was living on a farm at the time catching mice – an exhausting business!

After the death of Pharaoh Hatshepsut her stepson, Thutmose III, became pharaoh followed by his grandson, Amenhotep. Pharaoh Amenhotep had many sons, but his favourite was Thutmose, who

had been named after his grandfather.

"Little Thutmose, you are without doubt my best boy!" cooed Amenhotep.

His other sons were jealous of Thutmose. They feared that their father's "best boy" might inherit the crown, even though he was not the eldest.

"Daddy's boy!" they sneered at Thutmose.

Poor Thutmose, he loved his brothers and just wanted to be their friend.

"Daddy's boy! Daddy's boy! Daddy's boy!" they chanted.

Not only did Thutmose's brothers taunt him,
but they also tried to turn their father against him.

"Father! Thutmose broke your crown!" one lied.

"My best boy would never do such a thing,"
said their father.

"Father! Thutmose ate your supper!" another
accused.

"My best boy would never do such a thing,"
said their father.

"Father! Thutmose squashed your cat!"
announced another.

"My best boy would never do such a thing," said their father.

Indeed, Amenhotep could see no wrong in his best boy no matter what his other sons said. Frustrated by their inability to turn their father against Thutmose, the brothers became increasingly mean to him behind their father's back.

"You are not only a daddy's boy, but a friendless freak!" one of his brothers taunted.

"Daddy's best boy smells like the inside of a crocodile's mouth!" another laughed.

"Your bum is like the back end of a

hippopotamus!" was yet another brotherly jibe.

Pharaoh Amenhotep was too busy to be with his favourite son, so Thutmose tried to escape from his brothers' bullying by going hunting. One day when the court was at Memphis for a festival, Thutmose and two companions left to hunt gazelles

in the desert. They took their horses and rode until midday, when the heat forced them to stop and rest. Unable to entirely forget his brothers' jealous

taunts, Thutmose was too unhappy to lie still. He decided to leave his sleeping companions and go off and explore the great pyramids of Giza.

The pyramids were vast, but what fascinated Thutmose most was the head of a stone sphinx, sticking out of the sand. He thought it must be

a likeness of the god Harmachis so he prayed to
the god, asking that his brothers might leave him
in peace. Then, falling asleep in the shade of the

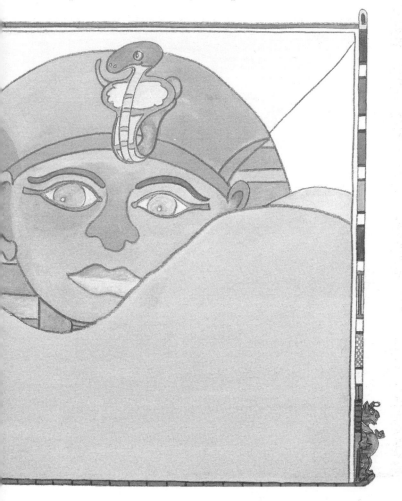

great sphinx, Thutmose had the strangest dream.
He dreamt that Harmachis asked him to clear away
all of the sand that covered him. In return the god
would make him pharaoh of Egypt, and make his
brothers honour and obey him.

When Thutmose woke, he remembered the dream and ordered offerings to be made to Harmachis and the sand to be cleared away from his likeness. He hoped that now his dream would come true and that his brothers might stop their teasing – but it was not to be.

"Where's daddy's best boy been?" his brothers jeered on his return. "Has he been to visit his hippo relatives?"

And so the taunting continued.

Some years later, Amenhotep died and Thutmose did become pharaoh of Egypt and – strange to tell – his brothers celebrated his coronation and never, ever teased him again!

"You can never tell with dreams." Pharaoh Thutmose smiled as he stroked his new little kitten, Rami. "Their predictions can come true when you least expect it!"

"You are so wise, Pharaoh Thutmose!" chorused his brothers.

> But with his death, I lost yet another life! I was mummified and put into a sarcophagus – I nearly didn't get out! Luckily I still had one more life left to live!

> You guessed it, my ticklers, after a life catching mice, I returned to court as the kitten of Pharaoh Thutmose.

Chapter Eight
THE BOY KING TUTANKHAMEN

If I was a boy and not a cat, I'd be like Tut. He was ever so wise for his age. Chin on paws! Listen in, my ticklers.

Sadly, Pharaoh Thutmose died after ruling Egypt for only ten years. He had been a good king and had brought peace and prosperity to Egypt. The people worried that their lives would change – and they were quite right to be worried! The crown had passed to Thutmose's youngest brother, Akhenaten, who was not only a warmonger but showed no respect for his people's ancient beliefs.

As soon as Akhenaten had the crown safely on his head, he decreed that the sun god Aten was

now the only god to be worshipped. He sacked all
of Amen Ra's priests and ordered the destruction of
the shrines and temples built in his honour.

"This is mine now. I can do with it what I will!"
Akhenaten declared, waving his arms around as
though he could encompass the whole of Egypt.

"Amen Ra and all his ancient mates are rubbish gods! If I see a single temple in their honour still standing by the next new moon, it'll be the end of you! Do you hear me, Vizier?"

"But Amen Ra is the god amongst gods, mighty Pharaoh," replied the vizier, nervously. "We have worshipped him since the beginning of time."

"Not any more, Aten is the *only* god now," retorted Akhenaten.

"You'll anger the other gods, most beloved Pharaoh," said the vizier, even more nervously.

"The other gods don't exist and nor will you if you don't hold your peace!" snapped Akhenaten.

"One god can't look after us all," whispered the vizier, who was now visibly shaking, unsure who he would anger most – Amen Ra or his pharaoh. Either way, he felt his life was in danger of being snuffed out at any minute.

"Aten has the power of all the gods within him ... and you're sacked!" announced Pharaoh Akhenaten.

"Sack me if you must, mighty Pharaoh," answered the vizier, gathering together every gram of his courage. "Only Amen Ra has the power of all the gods within him. You forget that at your peril – and probably your people's peril too!"

"Enough! Guards, strangle this heretic! Now!" ordered Akhenaten, before marching off to eat his lunch and say a prayer to Aten.

Pharaoh Akhenaten was obsessed with his new cult of Aten. He took little interest in governing Egypt and no interest at all in the welfare of his people. He thought only of building temples and shrines in honour of Aten.

"Pharaoh, the Nubians are about to invade us," his councillors warned him. "They are after more of our land."

"Well, give it to them. As long as I'm not planning to build a temple to Aten on the land, they can have it."

"But, Pharaoh, what about your people?" the councillors cried. "They don't want to be ruled by Nubians."

"Then let them fight the Nubians, just don't bother me about it," snapped Akhenaten. "Can't you see I'm busy designing another temple for the one and only god Aten?"

The people of Egypt were confused and angry at the loss of their ancient gods. They knew nothing about the god Aten, but they all knew and loved the stories of the ancient gods. The discipline and stability that worshipping the gods had given them was now slipping away and Egypt was falling into a state of disorder. Crime and violence increased and neighbour turned on neighbour, often for little or no reason.

"Neighbour, why are you killing me for two grains of wheat?" one man cried.

"Why not? There are no gods to anger except Aten – and he's an impostor!" came the reply.

With the whole of Egypt in a state of disarray, nobody felt any sadness when Akhenaten died suddenly, leaving his son Tutankhaten to become the new pharaoh. The people of Egypt were hugely

relieved, even though Tutanhkaten was a puny nine year old who walked with a stick. Anything would be better than Akhenaten ... or so the people thought!

"Hurrah, hurrah! Tut for pharaoh!" cried his people, laughing and celebrating with their neighbours once more.

"Egypt will be a mighty power once more!" cheered the delighted ministers.

Unfortunately, Tutankhaten did not have the wisdom that sometimes comes with age. He had been taught by his father Akhenhaten that Aten was the one and only god and, like a good son, he respected his father's beliefs.

At the beginning of his reign, Tutankhaten and his vizier Ay upheld his father's beliefs and continued promoting the worship of Aten. He carried on building shrines to Aten and punished those who

paid homage to the ancient gods, sometimes with death. Unlike his father Akhenhaten, Pharaoh Tutankhaten was not bad at heart and when he saw how unhappy this forced worship made his people, he wondered if his father might have been just a touch misguided.

"Do you think Dad could have been wrong about this god Aten, Ay?" he pondered.

"Possibly, but then again, possibly not," replied Ay, who was nervous of saying the wrong thing and being strangled on the spot.

"I think it is most possible," declared Tutankhaten. "Time for some changes!"

After two years in charge, wise young Pharaoh Tutankhaten changed his name to Tutankhamen in honour of Amen Ra and reinstated the priests and temples that honoured the ancient gods.

"Your father will be turning in his tomb!" his mother complained.

"Mother, I'm eleven years old and I'll do what I want, praise be to Ra!" replied Tutankhamen. "Besides, it is so much more uplifting when your people cheer you as you pass. Now, prepare the palace, because I plan to throw a few parties!"

Tutankhamen gave a series of lavish parties in honour of Amen Ra. He invited all the priests of Aten and representatives of every district of Egypt. He encouraged them to return to worshipping the ancient gods for the good of Egypt. After much wine, food and discussion, all were ready to reinstate the old gods – even the high priests of Aten!

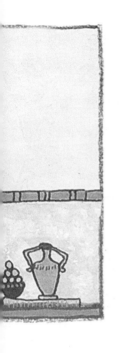

Following years of misery, the Egyptians now had the freedom to worship the gods of their ancestors. They were content once more and the country began to prosper. The people of Egypt praised their young pharaoh, who had given them back this freedom. They wished him a long life and a happy reign, though sadly this was not to be.

When Tutankhamen was only nineteen years old, he fell and fractured his thigh. Frail from

birth and also suffering from malaria, the young pharaoh quickly weakened. All the ancient gods were called upon to save the king but, in spite of all the prayers and sacrifices, Tutankhamen died.

The whole of Egypt mourned the passing of Pharaoh Tutankhamen who, in spite of his tender years, had ruled Egypt most wisely. After seventy days, Tutankhamen's body was placed in a huge tomb in the Valley of the Kings. On the outside of the tomb was inscribed a terrible curse: "Death shall come on swift wings to him that disturbs the peace of the king."

The tomb was filled with a vast hoard of treasures, including 130 walking sticks to aid Pharaoh Tutankhamen's journey to the next

life. So numerous and so valuable were the grave

goods, that several false chambers were constructed

to confuse any grave robbers. It is my belief that

the richness of the treasures was the Egyptians' way

of thanking the young pharaoh for reinstating
their ancient beliefs in Amen Ra and the other
wonderful gods.

Thanks be to Ra, I did not lose another life
and end up in Tut's tomb. For I only had
one life left and I was saving that!

Chapter Nine
CLEOPATRA, THE LAST PHARAOH OF EGYPT

So for one last time my ticklers, chin on paws!

Lucky is the storytelling cat whose last life coincides with the reign of Cleopatra, for she turned every day into a drama to be told.

Cleopatra was the much-loved daughter of Pharaoh Ptolemy XII of Egypt. It was often said that she was a great beauty, but in truth she was nothing

special to look at – even though she took
a daily bath in ass's milk, which she believed would
improve the texture of her skin. No, Cleopatra had
something of far greater value – she had an outstanding personality. She was also ambitious, very
clever and she wanted to be queen of Egypt.
What Cleopatra wanted, Cleopatra usually got!

After the death of her father in 51 BCE,
Cleopatra became joint ruler with her husband and
brother Ptolemy XIII. Was she pleased? No, not
Cleopatra. She wanted the throne all for herself!
Of course she did, Cleopatra didn't want to share
power with anyone – certainly not her brother!

"Isn't this fun, Cleo?" said her brother. "Now
we share power, we can both have our faces
on Egyptian coins. You on one side and me
on the other!"

"No, it is not fun, brother. We will have my face on both sides. You've got such an ugly mug," replied his sister. "And besides, I speak nine languages and all you speak is Greek! Actually," continued Cleopatra, not giving her brother a chance to say anything, "it is my opinion that both the coin and this throne are too small for the two of us. I suggest you go and find another throne. I hear the Nubians are in need of a ruler."

"You have to share this throne – I am the pharaoh of Egypt!" said Ptolemy, stamping his foot. "And you're just a feeble and ignorant woman!"

This was too much for Cleopatra, who was certainly not feeble or ignorant and probably twice, if not three times as clever and quick-witted as her brother. She decided that the only thing she could do would be to oust him and take the throne for herself – by force if necessary.

"Of course, I would only stab my brother in the back if it was for the good of Egypt," she explained to her pet leopard Arrow and her favourite cat, Rami. "One has to put one's country before all things."

Cleopatra began to make secret plans to steal the throne from Ptolemy.

"I know you're up to something," he muttered.

"Whatever it is, you won't get away with it!"

"Me, brother? Up to something? Never!"
Cleopatra smirked.

When the great Roman leader Julius Caesar
visited Egypt, Cleopatra decided to seek his help.
Ptolemy, realizing that Cleopatra was up to no
good, tried to prevent her from meeting Caesar.

"I need to have a word with Caesar ... alone!"
she said to Caesar's guards.

"No chance!" they replied. "Your brother, the pharaoh, has warned us about you. You might murder our great Caesar – or worse!"

"It's like that, is it?" growled Cleopatra. "Well, brother, two can play at that game."

Neither Ptolemy nor Caesar's guards were a match for Cleopatra. She returned to her rooms in the palace and, after dressing in her finest robes, made her slaves hide her in a rolled-up carpet. She then ordered them to deliver the carpet as a gift from her to Caesar.

"Gift for the mighty Caesar," proclaimed the slaves, as they approached the guards with their precious bundle held aloft.

The guards prodded and poked the carpet suspiciously but they could see nothing wrong with it. So, knowing how much Caesar loved a gift, they let the slaves through.

"Enter!" cried the guards. "You'll find mighty

Caesar down the passage and on the right."

As the slaves lay the carpet at Caesar's feet and began to unroll it – out popped Cleopatra! What an entrance, the queen of Egypt arriving in a rug! Caesar was completely captivated. From that moment on, he was unable to resist even Cleopatra's smallest demand. Within minutes he had agreed to help her steal the crown of Egypt from Ptolemy.

"Rid me of Ptolemy, oh mighty and deliciously handsome Caesar, and together we can rule the world!" she promised.

"Anything you say, my little rug," sighed Caesar. "Let's attack him when he next ventures down the Nile."

"Good plan, my mighty man!" cooed Cleopatra.

"Trouble comes in many guises," warned Caesar's guard, but Caesar was deaf to all but Cleopatra.

In the civil war that followed, Ptolemy was killed and Cleopatra became the sole ruler of Egypt. Caesar stayed in Egypt to celebrate their triumph and as time passed he began to forget his responsibilities in Rome – being with Cleopatra was so delightful to him. The pair had a stormy relationship, but as long as Caesar always gave Cleopatra her way, they were happy enough and eventually they had a son called Caesarion.

Cleopatra no longer felt threatened by her brother and began to feel that actually, Egypt was rather a small country to rule. She decided she should take over the world – or at least Rome! So in preparation, she decided to visit Rome with Caesar and Caesarion.

"Caesarion will be emperor of Rome and

pharaoh of Egypt," Cleopatra crowed. "It's only right he visits the country."

"He may be ruler one day, my little rug," replied Caesar, "but first we will rule both countries."

In Rome, the senators were shocked by the couple's growing ambition and after months of plotting, they assassinated Caesar. Fearing for her own life and that of Caesarion, Cleopatra fled back to Egypt.

Relieved to be safely back in Egypt, Cleopatra set about restoring her power, her reputation and her country's wealth.

"We must repair the canals so that the fields are watered. We must trade more. We must make Egypt the greatest country ever so that my name is praised across the world!" she declared.

"Oh mighty Pharaoh, you are so wise," said anyone who valued their life. "Happy was the day you returned to us."

"Yes, I know," said Cleopatra. "And I am wise enough to know that with Caesar gone, we need another friend in Rome."

Without a Roman ally, Cleopatra knew that she did not have the power to prevent Egypt from becoming part of the Roman Empire. She took a very long bath in ass's milk and then dressed herself as the goddess Isis! Looking quite magnificent and every bit the goddess, Cleopatra set sail for Tarsus to meet the handsome young Mark Antony, who now ruled Rome alongside Caesar's godson, Octavius.

When Mark Antony saw Cleopatra floating down the Nile towards him, dressed in her most goddess-like finery, he was captivated – like Caesar before him.

"Not even I, the great Mark Antony, can resist

such a wonder!" he declared.

"Of course not," said Cleopatra, thinking that
even without the power of Rome behind him,

Mark Antony was rather a fine catch!

Mark Antony immediately forgot Rome (and
his Roman wife) and went back to Egypt with

Cleopatra. He stayed with her for several years, abandoning both his duty to his country and his

wife, until the Roman leader Octavius declared war on the pair.

"This is just what I was trying to avoid," snapped Cleopatra. "I should have sent you back to Rome to murder Octavius months ago, then

we wouldn't be in this mess."

"Don't worry, my little Egyptian dove," soothed Mark Antony. "We'll soon have him running for his life!"

Cleopatra and Mark Antony met Octavius at sea and fought many fierce battles. It seemed that neither side would win until one day, in the midst of yet another battle, Cleopatra and her navy suddenly turned their ships and fled.

"Enough! Let's go home," Cleopatra ordered

her sailors. "I'm sick of being at sea!"

"Cleo, don't leave me," cried Mark Antony.

But his voice was lost on the wind and
Cleopatra sailed on. Instead of staying and
finishing the battle, Mark Antony turned his
ships and followed Cleopatra back to Egypt.

"Perfect!" gloated Octavius triumphantly. "I

believe that if the enemy ships turn and flee, I am the winner!"

Mark Antony landed in Egypt a broken man. He had betrayed his country for Cleopatra, and now she had betrayed him.

There was only one honourable thing to do. Mark Antony took out his sword. "You are the

only friend I have left," he wept, and fell on its

sharpened point so that it pierced him through.

Octavius was delighted at the death of Mark

Antony and rushed to capture Cleopatra. He could

hardly wait to parade her through the streets of all

the cities she had once ruled ... as his slave.

"How your people will laugh at you, now that

you're my prisoner," he gloated.

Cleopatra, the once proud queen of Egypt,

could never submit to such a fate. With the help
of her loyal slaves, she managed to escape to her
tomb. She dressed in her finest ceremonial robes
and then ordered an asp to be brought to her,
hidden in a basket of figs.

"Come, my pretty one, it is an honour to
bite the arm of a pharaoh," she whispered to the
creature.

Holding the serpent lovingly in her hands
she allowed it to bite her. As the asp released its

venom, Cleopatra lay back – she knew that the
bite of an asp would be fatal, but she also believed
that it would make her immortal. Maybe Cleopatra
was right, for with her death, Egypt became part
of the Roman Empire and so Cleopatra will always

be remembered as the last of Ancient Egypt's great pharaohs – as well as for her outstanding personality.

And as for me, my ticklers, the time has come for me to call upon Ra to take me back into the heavens, for I feel my ninth life slipping from me.

Like Cleopatra, I will always be remembered, but as Rami, Ra the Shining One's favourite cat – and the finest story-teller known in all of Ancient Egypt!

TEN TERRIFIC THINGS YOU NEVER KNEW ABOUT ANCIENT EGYPT
(And probably wish you didn't!)

1. The Ancient Egyptians were great farmers; they grew all their own food and kept livestock. It took 700 asses to provide enough milk for Cleopatra's daily bath!

2. They were also amazing inventors and created the very first hiero-glyphic writing that used pictures to represent words.

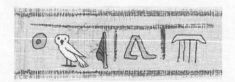

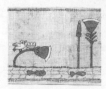
3. Luckily they also developed the very first type of paper (papyrus) which was made from thinly sliced reeds laid across each other.

4. Senet, the first board game, was invented by the Ancient Egyptians over 5,500 years ago. It had a board with three rows of ten, and two sets of pawns, but how to play it? No one knows!

5. Cats were the most-loved creatures (of course) and Egyptian temples were full of pampered cats. WARNING! You could be put to death for killing a cat!

6. When a pet cat died, the family would shave off their eyebrows – and howl in mourning! They might even have had their feline friend mummified.

7. Children married very young, so childhood was short. You could be married off as young as eight years old!

8. The Ancient Egyptians worshipped over 1,000 different gods and goddesses – you wonder how they managed to keep track of them all...

9. Men and women had equal rights, which was unusual in ancient civilizations. There was no such thing as a king or a queen – pharaoh was used for both genders. Both men and women wore make-up!

10. Mummies had their internal organs taken out and preserved in separate containers called canopic jars. There would be one each for the liver, intestines, stomach and lungs. Each jar had a protective god and they were stored in a special chest in the mummy's tomb.

GLOSSARY

ASP: a bad-tempered and venomous snake. Best avoided unless you've got a death wish or you're the mighty Cleopatra.

BEARD OF OFFICE: ceremonial symbol of power, which looked great on a male pharaoh but ridiculous on Hatshepsut. I loved her to bits, but not a good look!

BURIAL CHAMBER: room in a tomb where a dead body is laid. The larger and more highly decorated, the richer and more important the dead person. As in life, so in death.

CANALS: artificial waterways for navigation or irrigation. They required thousands of hours of slave labour to build and are not at all cat-friendly – nothing watery is!

CAT: cat, cat, cat, cat, cat! What a wonderful word for a simply delightful, cuddlesome, furry creature and Ra's favourite pet!

CEREMONIAL ROBES: smart clothes worn for state occasions. Unlike cats, humans have to dress up to look smart!

 COBRA: another nasty, venomous serpent-type creature to be avoided, especially if created out of sand and spittle

CURSE: to call on supernatural powers to harm someone. My Uncle Abasi had a curse put on him – he lost all his hair and grew an extra tail!

DESERT: an area of very dry, sandy land. Do not try to cross it in bare feet because you'll burn them. It's the truth! Ask any cat.

DUAT: hush! Only whisper this word, for it is the realm of the dead and if you disturb them they may come and haunt you!

EMBALMING: gross procedure for preserving a dead body that requires hooking your brain out through your nose!

EMPEROR: well, this is an obvious one – an emperor is the ruler of an … empire

FALSE CHAMBER: love these! They're completely pointless extra rooms built in tombs to confuse grave robbers. They don't – they just make the robbery take longer!

 FAMINE: this is a serious disaster – a severe shortage of fish and other food. My tummy shrinks at the fearful thought.

FLOOD: another cat-unfriendly disaster. Water spreads over land that should be dry and if you can't swim – or are a cat and just don't do water – you drown!

GIZA: rat- and pyramid-infested city on the Nile

GOD: male spirit or being that is worshipped – praise be to Ra, the Shining One, creator of life and my favourite god

GODDESS: female spirit or being that is worshipped – praise be to Bastet, the cat goddess, snake killer and my favourite goddess

GRAVE GOODS: treasure meant for a dead person to take with them into the next world. A painful subject, as pets (such as my good and most-treasured self) are often slaughtered and buried with these goods. It is hoped that we will end up purring on the knee of the dead person in the next world. Has yet to be proved...

GRAVE ROBBERS: a nasty bunch who rob the defenceless dead. Curses be upon them!

HIEROGLYPHS: even a cat can see that this is a totally beautiful and amazing form of picture writing!

MORTAL: a living being, such as a human being or a snake, that is subject to death. Unlike an immortal god who is not subject to death – even after nine lives!

MUMMY: either your mother or a person mummified and preserved after death. Remember that hook up the nose that drags your brains out?

NUBIANS: had an empire bordering Egypt. I helped them out with a rat infestation – nice lot and good fighters (the Nubians not the rats!).

PHARAOH: ruler of Ancient Egypt – can be a human or a god. Cats and other assorted creatures need not apply.

PYRAMID: monument with a square base and four sloping sides, often commissioned by a pharaoh who wants to look important. The bigger the pyramid, the larger the ego...

RIVER NILE: the longest, most beautiful river in the world. Full of delightful fishy food but watch out for those over-toothed crocodiles.

ROMANS: generally not mentioned by Egyptians as they saw fit to invade us. I believe they came from a city called Rome in Italy but it took them nearly 700 years to find their way back.

ROYAL BARGE: boat for the use of the pharaoh (or palace cat) for travelling on inland waterways

SACRIFICE: offering of a slaughtered animal (or human) to a god or goddess. Probably wise to do this now and then, the odd rat or mouse goes a long way to keeping those heavenly beings sweet.

SARCOPHAGUS: stone coffin, extremely hard to get out of if you want to cheat death and live another of your nine lives!

SCORPION: a type of spider (but you wouldn't know it) with lobster-like pincers and a nasty, spiteful, extremely painful sting in their tail

SECRET NAME: I can't tell you what it is, because it's a secret, but the god Nu (aka Nun) gave it to Ra and it was the source of all his power

 SPHINX: a mythical creature with the head of a human and the body of lion

TEMPLE: building used for worship (also a safe place for cats – kill a temple cat at your peril for the punishment is death!)

THEBES: ancient capital of Egypt, a city of stories, pharaohs and cats – quite beyond compare

TOMB: where dead bodies are stored, unless you are a person or cat of no importance, then you will be dropped into a hole in the desert – plop!

UNDERWORLD: land of the dead through which you must pass in order to travel to the heavens

 VALLEY OF THE KINGS: area of the city of Thebes where many great (and some not so great) pharaohs were buried

VENOM: poison from some snakes and scorpions. Not always fatal, but can be. Remember Cleopatra?

VIZIER: pharaoh's chief advisor and an important person to keep on the right side of. Every night the vizier reports to the pharaoh and you would not want him to report some misdemeanour of yours. Unless you want to visit the Duat!

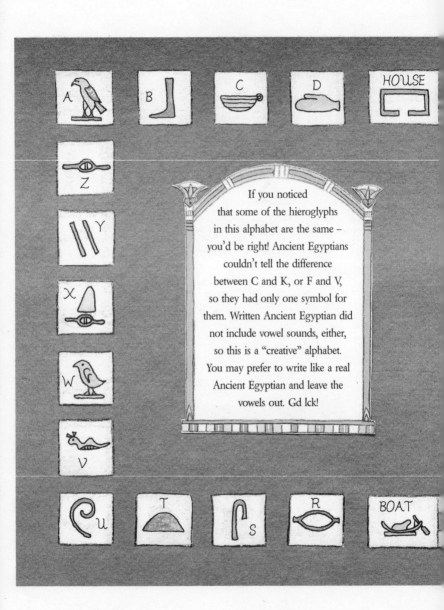

A

B

C

D

HOUSE

Z

Y

X

W

V

If you noticed that some of the hieroglyphs in this alphabet are the same – you'd be right! Ancient Egyptians couldn't tell the difference between C and K, or F and V, so they had only one symbol for them. Written Ancient Egyptian did not include vowel sounds, either, so this is a "creative" alphabet. You may prefer to write like a real Ancient Egyptian and leave the vowels out. Gd lck!

U

T

S

R

BOAT